More
Twenty-Minute Tales

D1513916

Enid Blyton

More Twenty-Minute Tales

A DRAGON BOOK

GRANADA

London Toronto Sydney New York

Published by Granada Publishing Limited in 1972
Reprinted 1975, 1978, 1980, 1982, 1983

ISBN 0 583 30185 1

First published in Great Britain by
Methuen & Co Ltd 1940
Copyright © Enid Blyton 1940

Granada Publishing Limited
Frogmore, St Albans, Herts AL2 2NF
and
36 Golden Square, London W1R 4AH
515 Madison Avenue, New York, NY 10022, USA
117 York Street, Sydney, NSW 2000, Australia
60 International Blvd, Rexdale, Ontario, R9W 6J2, Canada
61 Beach Road, Auckland, New Zealand

Printed and bound in Great Britain by
Cox & Wyman Ltd, Reading
Set in Monotype Times

This book is sold subject to the condition that it
shall not, by way of trade or otherwise, be lent,
re-sold, hired out or otherwise circulated
without the publisher's prior consent in any
form of binding or cover other than that in
which it is published and without a similar
condition including this condition being imposed
on the subsequent purchaser.

Granada ®
Granada Publishing ®

Contents

1: *The Big Blue Cat*

Beauty was a big blue Persian cat. Her name was a good one, for she certainly was beautiful. Her tail was very thick and fluffy, her eyes were a deep yellow, her whiskers were very long, and her coat was simply lovely – a deep grey-blue, very silky and long.

Beauty belonged to Betty. Betty wasn't very old, but she knew how to look after her pets. She had two – Goldie her canary, and Beauty her cat. She cleaned Goldie's cage out each day and gave him fresh food and water, and she brushed Beauty's lovely coat and saw that she had plenty of milk to drink and a warm basket to sleep in at night.

One day Betty came home very much excited.

"Mummy!" she cried, "there's to be a Cat Show in the next town soon! Do you think Beauty would win a prize if I show her there? Oh, wouldn't it be lovely if she did!"

"I'm sure she would!" said Mummy, quite excited too. "Yes, let's enter Beauty's name, Betty. It would be fine if she won a prize. She really is a beautiful cat, and you keep her very nicely."

"If she wins a prize I shall use the money to buy her a new basket," said Betty. "She needs a new one. Beauty, Beauty, come here! I'm going to give you an extra brushing every day so that you will look really nice on the show day."

Beauty let Betty do anything she wanted. She loved the little girl and followed her about all day. Betty brushed her, combed her, gave her fresh milk morning and afternoon and bought her a beautiful blue ribbon to wear.

At last the show day came near. It was the very next day! How excited Betty was! You should have seen Beauty, too, She looked the loveliest cat in the world! Betty

8

was quite sure she would win the first prize.

And then a most dreadful thing happened. It was like this – Betty was taking Beauty for a walk down the lane, when a strange dog came by. Beauty was frightened, and fled away down the lane by herself. She ran up a tree and stayed there until the dog had gone.

Betty didn't see where she went. She called her and hunted for her, but it wasn't a bit of good. Beauty was up the tree and she didn't even mew, for fear that dog should come back again.

When at last she did come down, a car was passing by. The people in the car saw the beautiful cat and stopped. One of the men jumped out, picked up the surprised cat and hopped back into the car with her. At that moment Betty came by, still calling for Beauty. Beauty mewed and struggled and tried to jump out to go to her little mistress.

But the man wouldn't let her go. Betty saw Beauty and ran towards the car.

"You've got my cat! You've got Beauty!" she cried. "Give her to me!"

But the wicked man started up his car and off he went down the lane at top speed, taking Beauty with him! He had stolen her! He saw that she was a valuable cat and he thought he might be able to sell her to some one and get some money for himself.

Wasn't it dreadful? Betty didn't know what to do. She ran home, crying, and burst into the kitchen, where Mummy was making cakes for tea.

"Mummy! Mummy! Some one's stolen Beauty! They've taken her away in a car! Oh, Mummy! She'll be so unhappy! And it's the show day to-morrow!"

Mummy took Betty on her knee and comforted her. She was very upset too, for she loved Beauty as much as Betty did.

"Darling, don't cry," she said. "We'll soon get her back. I'll telephone to the police station and tell the policemen all about it. They will catch the robber and get Beauty for you again."

"Will they get her in time for the show?" asked Betty.

"I don't know, dear. I hope so," said

Mummy. "Did you notice the number of the car?"

"Oh, Mummy, I never thought of looking for it!" said Betty. "I was so upset about Beauty that I didn't think of anything else. Oh, how silly I was not to look at the car! I don't even know what colour it was."

"That *is* a pity," said Mummy. "Never mind. I'll go and telephone to the police station now."

Betty couldn't eat any tea. She wandered about thinking of poor Beauty and wondering where she was.

"Oh, *I* do hope the policemen get her back in time for the show," she said to herself a hundred times.

A big policeman came to the house on his bicycle. He asked Betty a lot of questions about the man and the car, and poor Betty couldn't answer any of them. She hadn't noticed anything at all except Beauty being taken away.

The policeman was very kind. He wrote a lot of things down in his notebook, but when Betty asked him if he could get

Beauty back before the show began the next afternoon, he shook his head.

"I'm afraid not, little Missy," he said. "But cheer up, we'll get Beauty back some time!"

Betty cried when she went to bed that night. She was so unhappy. She missed Beauty, and she was dreadfully disappointed to think that her lovely cat wouldn't be in the show after all. She was so proud of her, and now nobody would see her.

Poor Beauty was just as unhappy. She had been taken a long way away in the car. At last the man driving drew up at a little house, and he and the other man and a woman got out and went indoors. They took Beauty with them.

"She's a lovely cat," said one of the men. "We can sell her for two or three pounds!"

"Where shall we put her?" said the woman. "Mind she doesn't scratch. She's very frightened and angry."

Beauty did try to scratch. She knew that these people had no business to take her away and she wanted to get back to Betty. But they wouldn't let her go.

Beauty was put in a little attic at the top of the house. They gave her a rug to lie on and put a saucer of milk for her. They shut the window fast and then went out and shut the door. Beauty was a prisoner.

The big cat prowled all round the room to find a way of escape. The window was quite shut. The door wouldn't open, although Beauty jiggled at the handle. It was locked on the other side. Beauty mewed more and more loudly, but nobody came. Nobody even heard her, shut up at the top of the house.

Beauty scratched at the door. She scratched all the paint off, but it wasn't a bit of good, she couldn't get through that door. She was hungry, but she wouldn't taste the milk. She was tired, but she wouldn't lie down. She must GET OUT!

But how could she? Poor Beauty! She wanted her little mistress Betty, she was lonely and frightened. There was nobody to pet and comfort her. She was miles away from home.

After a long time the woman opened the door and came in. Beauty tried to run out of the door, but she closed it quickly.

"Oh, no, you don't escape as easily as that," said the woman. "Oh, look at all the paint scraped off the door! You naughty cat! I'll smack you for that!"

She stooped to smack Beauty and the frightened cat put out her claws and scratched the woman all down her arm.

"Oh! Oh!" cried the woman, in alarm. "You wild creature! I won't stay in the room alone with you another minute!"

She rushed out of the room and locked the door. Beauty was left alone again. She prowled round and round the little room, and at last the daylight went and it was dark.

Everything was quiet. Then suddenly there came a tiny noise. Beauty pricked up her ears and listened. She didn't know what it was, but she thought it must be a mouse.

It wasn't. It was a tiny bit of soot falling down the chimney. Beauty padded over to the fireplace and listened. Another tiny bit of soot fell down. Beauty squeezed into the fireplace itself and looked up the chimney. At the top she saw a star shining, and smelt the open air.

Why, here was a way of escape! If only she could climb up the chimney and get out on the roof!

Beauty began to climb up the sooty chimney. Her claws were long and sharp and she held on tightly. Once or twice she slipped, but she soon took hold again and climbed upwards once more.

She squeezed herself right out of the top of the chimney and looked round. She was on the roof of the house! Beauty was quite used to roofs. She had often walked on the roof at home and sunned herself there. She wasn't at all frightened.

Suddenly she heard a noise down the chimney. She popped her head in and listened. It was the man and the woman in the room below. They had come in to see the cat and had found her gone. And they could NOT imagine where she had gone to – until they saw some soot in the fireplace, and then they guessed.

"That wretched cat has climbed up the chimney!" said the man angrily. "Whoever would have thought it was clever enough to do that! Well, we can't catch it now!"

Beauty didn't wait to hear any more. She slipped round the chimney, padded down the sloping roof, jumped down to another roof below, ran to a high wall, jumped on to that and then leapt down to the ground. She was safe!

Beauty wanted to go home – but she didn't know where she was! She didn't know in what direction her home lay – in front of her, or behind, to the right of her or to the left. Never mind she meant to go home that night!

Most animals have a strange magic sense, when they are lost, of knowing which way to go. Beauty knew she had only to lie quietly for a moment and think of her home and then she would suddenly know which way to go.

She lay down on a grassy patch and kept quiet. She thought of her home and of Betty, and she longed to be back with her little mistress again. And as she lay there she felt as if something were pulling her to the right. She must run to the right Her home lay in that direction.

Who told Beauty that? Nobody knows! But all cats and dogs can find their way home from a strange place, if only they will not get too frightened. Beauty was not frightened any longer. She was only afraid when she was locked up in some place. When she was out in the open she was afraid of nothing.

She ran over the grass to the right. She came to a fence and jumped over it. Then on she went into the night. Sometimes she came to a wall, a stream or a house and had to turn out of her way. But somehow or other she managed to take the right turnings each time, and whenever she felt lost, she simply lay down and thought of her home. Then she would feel as if something was pulling her to the right or to the left, and off she would run in the right direction.

She went for miles and miles. She was tired and hungry. Her feet became sore with running, for a cat's paws are not hard like a dog's, meant for running on. They are soft and velvety. But Beauty didn't mind. She meant to get home somehow or other, no matter how many miles it was.

The night passed on. The stars were pale when the dawn came. The sun made the eastern sky pink and gold. It rose like a big golden ball and Beauty was glad, because now she could see better where she was going.

She ran through a town where nobody was up. She ran through a village where only a baby was awake, crying for its bottle. She ran through dewy fields and down green lanes where the birds were beginning to sing to the morning sun.

And at last, when postmen were going from house to house and milkmen were finishing their early rounds, Beauty knew where she was! She was in the village at the end of which was her own home. How glad she was!

Betty had awakened early that morning. She had dreamed all night long of poor Beauty, and as soon as she woke she remembered what had happened. She jumped out of bed and ran to Beauty's basket, hoping that perhaps the policeman had brought her back in the night. But the basket was empty.

Betty's eyes filled with tears. It was the day of the Cat Show, and she had no cat to take, after all. She dressed herself slowly and went down to breakfast. Daddy and Mummy were already there.

"Cheer up, darling," said Daddy, when he saw her tears. "Crying won't bring Beauty back, you know."

"I know, Daddy," said Betty. "But it's the show to-day, and I'm so dreadfully disappointed not to have my lovely old Beauty."

Now just as they all sat down to breakfast there came a mewing outside the the window. Yes, it was Beauty, just arrived, tired and hungry, but *so* happy to be back. Betty jumped up from her chair in a trice and rushed to the window, shouting: "That's Beauty! I know it is!"

And so it was! The cat sat under the window, waiting to be let in, and as soon as Betty flung up the pane Beauty jumped in. How Betty hugged her! And you should have seen how Beauty rubbed against the little girl's cheek, and heard how she purred! Why, you couldn't hear yourself speak!

'Oh, Beauty, darling Beauty! Where have you been?" cried Betty. "Oh, your poor feet are so tired! And your fur is wet with dew and full of all sorts of bits! Are you hungry? You shall have a lovely breakfast!"

Mummy and Daddy were just as pleased as Betty to have Beauty back. Mummy fetched some milk from the kitchen and some fish too, and put them down for Beauty. She drank all the milk and ate all the fish! She purred and purred and purred.

"Oh, Mummy, I'll be able to take her to the show after all!" cried Betty suddenly. "I'd forgotten all about it! It isn't till three o'clock this afternoon. Do you think I can take Beauty?"

"Well, you'll have to clean her up a good bit," said Mummy. "And the poor creature is very tired. She must have run for miles, all night long, to get back home. Let her have a lovely long sleep, Betty, and then see how she is when she wakes up."

So Betty put Beauty into her basket and the tired cat fell fast asleep. How she slept! She slept all the morning and woke up at dinner-time. She ate all the dinner Betty gave her and then began to wash herself.

"Mummy, she seems all right now," said Betty. "Do you think I could brush her and make her pretty, and then take her to the show?"

"Yes, I think so," said Mummy. "She doesn't seem any the worse for her adventure."

So Betty brushed and combed Beauty's lovely coat. She tied a fine blue ribbon round her neck, and then gave her tail one last brush. Beauty looked simply lovely!

Daddy took Betty and Beauty in his car to the big hall in the next town where the Cat Show was to be held. Betty had her ticket and Beauty's and she found the little bench where Beauty was to sit. It was great fun to see all the other cats. Beauty curled up and went to sleep, for she was still rather tired.

The time came for the judges to see all the cats. Beauty woke up. They looked at her snow-white teeth. They stroked her head. They tickled her under the chin. They looked at her claws, and admired her beautiful eyes. Then they passed on to the next cat.

Betty's heart was beating fast. Would they give Beauty a prize or not? Perhaps she was too tired to get a prize. She didn't look tired to Betty, but maybe the judges could see more than she could. Goodness, how fast her heart was beating!

Presently along came the judges again, with some coloured tickets in their hands. The blue ticket said: "First Prize" on it, the red ticket said: "Second Prize", the green one said: "Third Prize" and the yellow one said "Fourth Prize".

And whatever do you think! Beauty had the blue ticket – the First Prize! It was pinned up beside her, and you should have seen Betty's face! It was as red as a tomato, and Betty hugged Beauty for joy.

But that wasn't all. There was a special prize given for the most beautifully kept cat, and Beauty won that too! The judges said they could see how well brushed and combed Beauty's coat was, and they knew how carefully Betty must have looked after her cat to make her so lovely. So they gave Beauty the special prize as well. Wasn't it exciting.

Daddy was there, of course, and he was so pleased with Betty and Beauty. The First Prize was worth two whole pounds and Daddy said that Betty must spend one of the pounds on herself, because she deserved it. The other pound she could keep for Beauty, and buy her a new rug and basket. The special prize was a silver mug with a cat's head carved on the handle. Betty was very proud of it.

She and Daddy and Beauty went home to show Mummy the prize ticket and the lovely silver mug. Mummy hugged Betty in delight.

"Well, you deserve it all, darling," she said. "It isn't many children who look after and love their pets as well as you do. I'm proud of you!"

"And *I'm* proud of Beauty!" said Betty happily. "Oh, Mummy, wasn't it a good thing Beauty came back this morning! I'd have been so unhappy if she hadn't. Beauty, you are a clever cat to find your way home, and I think you are just the loveliest and darlingest cat in the whole world!"

"Purrrrrrrrrrrr!" said Beauty rubbing her head against her mistress's legs. "Purrrrrrrrrrrr!"

I'm sure that meant: "You're the nicest little girl in the world!" Don't you think so?

2: *The Magic Toffee*

"Let's go up to Pixie Hill for a walk to-day," said Harry to Joan. "It's a long time since we went there, and we don't know it very well."

"I wonder why it's called Pixie Hill?" said Joan. "Perhaps the fairy folk lived there once upon a time. Yes, do let's go, Harry – it would be fun!"

So off they went together It was Saturday, so there was no school. The sun was shining, and it was just the day for exploring.

They took the little path that wound up the hillside. They saw the rabbits peeping at them, and heard the larks singing. Soon they got very hot, and Joan longed to sit down and have a rest.

"Let's leave this path and take that little

narrow one over there," she said, pointing. "Then, when we come to a shady spot we'll sit down and have a rest."

"It doesn't look much more than a rabbit-path, Joan," said Harry. "Still, it may lead somewhere. Come on!"

They went along the narrow path, and at last came to a birch-tree, whose branches cast a cool shade. The children threw themselves down on the grass and lay looking up into the leaves. It was very quiet. Only a lark could be heard singing, and a yellow-hammer crying: "Little bit of bread and no cheese!"

But then the children thought they heard another noise – a little humming sound. Not like a bee – but like some one humming a happy tune.

"Doesn't that sound like some one humming!" said Harry, sitting up. "But who can be near here? I didn't see any one near by, did you, Joan?"

"No," said Joan. "Let's just listen."

So they listened – and suddenly the humming stopped, and a small, high voice began to sing a queer song:

Peppermints and toffee-balls,
Candies pink and green,
Barley-sugar, chocolate,
Best you've ever seen!
Liquorice, marshmallows, too,
Lovely sugar-mice,
Sweets to bite and sweets to suck,
Everything that's nice!

"Goodness!" said Joan, startled. "That's a funny song, isn't it, Harry? I wonder who's singing it?"

"It makes me feel very hungry," said Harry. "I'd love to have some toffee, wouldn't you?'

"Let's go and see who's singing," said Joan, excited. "It might be a pixie."

They jumped up and ran towards the clump of bushes from which the song seemed to come, and when they peeped round it, they saw the most surprising sight.

Nestling right into the hillside, all alone, was a sweet-shop It was such a funny, oldfashioned one The windows were criss-crossed with strips of lead, just like the very old cottages in Harry's village. The little shop leaned sideways as if it were tired, and the chimneys were as crooked as could be.

Standing at the door, singing his curious song, was a little fat man, with small wings growing at the back of his neck. He wore a tunic of red, and tight hose of brown, and on his head was a pointed cap with little silver bells at the tip. There wasn't any doubt at all but that he was one of the pixie folk.

Joan was half frightened. She had never seen a fairy of any sort before. But Harry wasn't a bit afraid. He went boldly up to the little fat man and spoke to him.

"Can we buy some of your sweets?"

"Certainly," said the pixie, and he went inside his shop. Harry followed him, and Joan peeped in, too. What an exciting shop! There were dozens of tall bottles crammed with queer-looking sweets. Pink and white sugar mice sat on a shelf, and to Joan's enormous surprise they ran about from place to place just as if they were real, live mice.

"What sweets would you like?" asked

the little man politely. "I've some fresh-made peppermint to-day, if you like that."

"No, I don't like it much," said Harry, feeling in his pocket for a penny. "What about toffee?"

"I've some Toffee-Letters," said the pixie, and he reached down a big bottle, crammed with queer-shaped pieces of toffee. Harry looked at them, and to his surprise he saw that they were in the form of alphabet letters!

"Ooh, those are fine," he said. "I've never seen Toffee-Letters before. I'll have a pennyworth, please."

The pixie weighed out a big bagful in his shining scales. He gave them to Harry and took his penny.

"It's magic toffee," he said. "Be careful, won't you?"

Harry was most excited to hear it was magic toffee. He thanked the pixie and then ran out of the shop with Joan. The two children looked carefully at the Toffee-Letters. Except that the toffee was in the shape of letters, it didn't seem any different from the toffee they bought at home.

"I'm not going to have any," said Joan. "It might do something strange to me – make me big or little, or something like that. Don't you have any either, Harry."

' All right," said Harry. "I won't. I don't want anything strange to happen to me any more than you do!"

But, you know, Harry was one of those children who simply *must* eat sweets if they have some. And presently his hand slipped into the bag and he took out a toffee.

"I'm just going to taste it," he said to Joan. "If it tastes horrid, I won't eat it – or if it makes me feel funny I won't eat it either. Look, it's the letter H."

He tasted it. My goodness me, what a delicious taste it had! Like all the nicest sweets of the world put together! As soon as Harry tasted it he popped it right into his mouth and began to eat it. Oh, it was simply lovely.

"Joan, do have a Toffee-Letter," he said,

offering her the bag. "They're glorious! I don't feel a bit magic or strange."

But Joan said no. She liked toffee, but she wanted to be quite sure there was nothing wrong with those Toffee-Letters before she ate any.

Harry finished his letter H, and then popped his hand in the bag for another toffee. He took one out and looked at it. It was the letter E this time.

It tasted just as delicious as the first toffee, and Harry made up his mind that every Saturday he would go up Pixie Hill and buy his sweets at the funny little shop. If the toffee tasted so nice, the chocolate and the barley-sugar would be simply splendid.

He put his hand in the bag for another toffee. Joan looked at the letter he brought out. It was N this time. There seemed to be nearly all the letters of the alphabet in the bag. It was a very good pennyworth.

The children were climbing up the hill when Joan first noticed something rather queer about Harry. He was in front, and she happened to look at his bare legs.

"You've got some feathers stuck to your legs, Harry!" she called. "They do look funny!"

Harry stopped and looked at his legs. He tried to brush the feathers off – but they wouldn't go. He tried again, and then he look most astonished.

"Look, Joan," he said. "They're *growing* on my legs! They won't come off! Why ever is that?"

"Oh, Harry, it must be the magic in that toffee," said Joan, looking frightened. "Oh, dear, what is happening to you? Don't eat any more toffee, Harry, in case something else happens."

"Look!" said Harry, holding out his hands. "I've got brown feathers growing on my hands, too! I can't understand it. We'd better go back to that sweet-shop and ask the little fat man what to do. I can't go home with feathers all over me!"

They hurried down the hill and took the little narrow path to the sweet-shop again. The pixie was outside, humming his song once more. He was surprised to see the children again.

"Do you want some more sweets?" he asked.

"No," said Harry. "Look at my hands! And my legs! They've suddenly grown feathers and I want to know why. I can't go home like this!"

"Well, didn't I tell you that the toffee was magic?" asked the pixie. "I warned you."

"How is it magic?" said Harry, puzzled. "Does any one who eats it grow feathers, then?"

"Oh, no," said the pixie. "The letters are bewitched, so that if you eat F, A, T, for instance, you at once begin to grow fat. If you eat B, E, E, T, L, E, you change into a beetle. And so on. I don't know what letters you ate, but it's quite plain that you've started the magic working."

"He ate first an H, then E, then N," said Joan. "Oh, my goodness, that spells HEN! He's turning into a hen."

"Yes, that's right," agreed the pixie looking closely at Harry. "Those are hen's feathers on his hands and legs. He'll grow a red comb on his head soon, and feathers

33

all down his front. Then he'll grow a beak, and his arms will change into wings Then. . ."

"Oh, be quiet!" cried Joan, almost crying. "I don't want him to change into a silly hen! Take the magic away at once, pixie man."

"But, my goodness me, I can't do that!" said the sweet-shop man, looking surprised. "Why, it's tremendously powerful magic. I told you the toffees were enchanted, you know. If you didn't know what I meant, you should have asked me. Then you could have eaten RICH or GOOD or STRONG, and you would have been any of these things – instead of being so foolish as to eat HEN!"

"Well, what are we to do, then?" asked Joan. "Harry can't go on changing into a hen. Some one must stop him."

"Nobody can stop him," said the pixie, solemnly. "Nobody at all. I tell you, the magic is too powerful. Not even the King of Fairyland can stop Harry turning into a hen, or change him to his own shape once *he* is a hen!"

Joan began to cry. Harry tried to cry too, and to his alarm he clucked, instead of crying. How he wished he had asked about the magic in the toffees when he had bought them.

Joan threw her arms around her brother, and comforted him. She saw that a little red comb was beginning to grow under his golden hair, and she wondered whatever she could do for him.

"Isn't there anybody wise enough to tell Harry how to stop the magic?" she asked. "Tell me the names of some wise folk, and I'll go to them."

"Well," said the pixie, doubtfully, "there's the Wizard Knowalot. He lives the other side of the Yellow Hill. Then there's the Wise Woman Think-Hard. She lives underground. But if they can't help you, no one can."

"How can I get to the Wizard Know-alot?" asked Joan.

"I'll get the Green Bird to take you," said the little fat man. He took a whistle from his pocket and blew three times on it. As he blew the last time there came the whir of great wings, and a strange green bird, with an enormously long tail, dropped down to the ground.

"Get on," said the pixie man. The children climbed on his back. The pixie pointed to the west.

"Take them to the Wizard Knowalot," he commanded. At once the bird rose and flew off, with Harry and Joan clinging tightly to him. It was most exciting. The Green Bird flew steadily and swiftly for ten minutes and then Joan saw a curious Yellow Hill, very steep, with a little flat piece on top, on which was a perfectly round house.

The Green Bird flew down, and the children climbed off. Harry looked more feathery than ever, and Joan did hope that the wizard would cure him quickly.

They knocked at the door and it flew open. The room inside was enormous – indeed it looked as big as three cottages! Joan couldn't think how such a big room could be in such a small cottage. The wizard was at the end of it, stirring something in a big iron pot over a fire. The fire had strange green flames, very lovely.

"What do you want?" asked the wizard. "I'm busy."

"Oh, please don't be busy for a little while," begged Joan. "Look, here is my brother, who is changing into a hen because he ate Toffee-Letters with magic in them. Will you stop the magic and cure him!"

"*Im*-possible, im*poss*ible, quite impossible!" said the Wizard Knowalot, blinking at Harry. "Nobody can cure him."

"Oh, do try," begged Joan, crying.

"Can't," said the wizard, stirring vigorously. "Just can't be done. As I said before, Impossible!"

Joan looked at him in despair. Then she remembered what the pixie had said about the Wise Woman underground. Perhaps *she* would be able to help.

"Well, could you tell me where the Wise Woman lives?" she asked. "I'll go and ask her for help."

"Go, by all means," said the wizard politely. "Do you see that trap-door in my floor? Lift it up and go down the steps. Ask the mole who lives down there to guide you to Dame Think-Hard. Good-bye."

Joan lifted up the trap door he pointed to. There were steps going downwards. She and Harry climbed down and came to a little dark red door. It opened as they came near and a mole peeped out, dressed in a green shawl and a blue skirt, with glasses on her nose.

"Would you please take us to the Wise Woman Think-Hard?" asked Joan, hoping that Harry wouldn't change into a hen before they reached the Wise Woman. The mole nodded, and led them down a dark, winding passage which had candles stuck here and there to light the way. It was all very mysterious.

At last they reached a big glass door, and by the side was a brass plate with "Wise Woman" printed on it. They rang the bell and the door opened. The mole waved goodbye and ran off.

Harry and Joan walked into the queer room through the door. It was very misty, and blue and green smoke floated about everywhere, making it difficult to see things. But Joan could just make out an old woman sitting in a tall chair, knitting fast.

"Good day, my dears!" she said. "So you've come about those Toffee-Letters, have you?"

"How did you know?" asked Joan in astonishment.

"Ah, by my magic," said the old dame, smiling. "But I'm afraid I'm not clever enough to help you. The magic is too strong."

"But if you're clever enough to knit these clouds of green and blue smoke, surely you are wise enough to help poor Harry," said Joan. The old woman went on knitting the long streamers of smoke, and shook her head.

"My strongest magic is in this smoke," she said. "Let him sniff it and wrap it round him. It may do him good, but I doubt it."

Harry eagerly sniffed up the smoke and wrapped the misty veils round his feathery shoulders. But alas, it didn't alter him one bit – he was just as feathery as ever!

"There you are!" said Think-Hard. "I told you I couldn't help him. He shouldn't have eaten those sweets so foolishly."

Joan took hold of Harry's arm and turned to go. She was very sad and so was Harry.

"You can go out of that door, if you like," said the Wise Woman, pointing to a door that suddenly appeared on the opposite side. "It's nearer to your home."

Joan opened it and she and Harry went out. To their enormous surprise they were back on Pixie Hill again!

"How funny!" said Joan. "Look, Harry, we're on the path that leads home again!"

"Cluck, cluck," said Harry, and Joan looked at him in alarm. He was growing a beak now! Oh dear, dear, dear, whatever in the world could be done?

Then, because she loved her brother so very much, Joan thought harder than she had ever done in her life – and a most wonderful thought came into her head! She knew a way of saving Harry from turning into a hen! Yes, she really thought she did! No, she couldn't stop the magic –

but she could change it into something that didn't matter!

What was her wonderful thought! *You* could think of it too, if you tried. It seemed so easy when she had thought of it.

"Harry darling!" she cried. "I know! I know! You've eaten H. E. N, haven't you, and you're turning into a hen. Well, see if you've got the letters R and Y in your toffee-bag. If you eat those you'll have eaten H, E, N, R, Y, which spells Henry, and that's your real name – only we call you Harry instead!"

Harry stared at his excited little sister. Then he put his hand into his pocket and pulled out the sweet-bag. Yes, there were the letters R and Y there. Joan popped the R into his mouth and made him eat it. Then she popped the Y in.

"Now you've eaten HENRY, not HEN!" she cried. "The magic ought to turn you back into yourself, and make you Henry again, instead of a silly, feathery old hen!'

Sure enough, the feathers began to fall off Harry's arms and legs. The red comb on his head disappeared. His voice came back and he could speak instead of clucking. He was Henry, her own brother! Joan was so delighted that she cried for joy, and Harry hugged his clever little sister as if he would never let her go.

"I'm all right, I'm all right!" he cried. "But, Joan – do you think you'd better call me Henry, now, instead of Harry – or the magic might do something funny again. My name really *is* Henry, so it wouldn't seem strange to any one. Oh, Joan, aren't you clever. You're wiser than the wizard, cleverer than the Wise Woman!"

They went home together. Harry threw the rest of the sweets away, for he wasn't going to eat any more of those magic Toffee-Letters. He didn't want to meddle with magic any more!

They told their mother all that had happened, but she said she really couldn't believe it.

"Well, we'll take you up to the little pixie sweet-shop to-morrow, and show you the toffee," said Joan. So the next day they started off with Mother. They took the little narrow path again – but this time it led to a big rabbit-hole! How queer! There was no sweet-shop at all.

"Oh, where has it gone?" cried Joan. "It was just exactly here, I know, Mummy. And oh, look! Here's an empty sweet-bag! That just shows you there was a sweet-shop here, doesn't it, Mummy? We'll come back again and find the little shop another day. *It's* sure to be there *one* day!"

If you happen to find it yourself, be careful of those Toffee-Letters, won't you? Make up your mind what you want to be, and then eat the word in toffee – but be sure you spell it right!

3: *Snip-Snap the Enchanter*

Mummy had been to see old Mrs. Brown at the farm, and when she got back she called Leslie and Jean to her.

"My dears," she said. "I've lost the dear little pearl brooch with M for Mother on it, that you gave me for my birthday. I'm so unhappy about it. I lost it somewhere by the stile that leads to the farm. I heard it drop, but when I looked for it I couldn't see it anywhere. Do you think you could go and look for it? I'd be glad to have it back."

"Yes, we'll go now!" said Leslie. "Cheer up, Mummy, I expect we'll find it!"

Off they went to the stile that led to the farm. They began to hunt, but no matter how hard they looked there wasn't a sign of that brooch anywhere. Suddenly they heard what sounded like a little laugh. They turned round, and to their great surprise they saw a small brownie standing by a bush, laughing at them.

Neither Jean nor Leslie had ever seen a brownie before, but they knew what he was because of the pictures in their books at home. They were so astonished that they couldn't say a word.

"Ho, ho!" said the small man. "I know what you're looking for! A pearl brooch with M on!"

"Yes, we are!" cried Jean. "Oh, have you found it? Do give it to us if you have."

"Yes, I've found it," said the brownie. "I saw it drop from your mother's dress and it fell near my bush. So I put my hand out and took it! It's just what I want for my new coat!"

"But you must give it back," said Leslie, angrily. "It doesn't belong to you."

"If I give it back, will you do something for me?" asked the brownie.

"It depends what it is," said Jean. "What do you want?"

"Well, it's like this," said the brownie, coming nearer to them. "I want three yellow feathers from the Hoodle Bird who lives in the Enchanter Snip-Snap's castle. I've got a fine blue hat and it just wants three yellow feathers in it to make it the finest hat in Brownie-Town. But Snip-Snap is cross with me for making faces at him last time he went by, so I don't like to go to his castle for the feathers, though the Hoodle Bird would give them to me all right. Will you go to get the feathers for me? Then you shall have back the brooch!"

Jean and Leslie listened in astonishment. What an adventure! Fancy going to an enchanter's castle and asking a Hoodle Bird for three feathers! Well, well, well!

"Shall we go?" said Leslie to Jean.

"Ooh, yes, let's!" she said. The brownie looked pleased.

"You'll have to come with me, and I'll show you the way," he said. "Get under this bush."

The children squeezed under the bush and to their great astonishment they saw a trapdoor there. The brownie opened it and the children went down some steps. They found themselves in a little underground house, very small and tidy, lighted by large glow-worms in round lamps. It was very strange.

The brownie opened a door at the back of the underground room.

"Come along," he said. "This way."

They followed him out into a passage. All along it were other doors and on them were pinned cards with names written on them. Jean read some of them. They were most exciting.

"Sandy Rabbit" was written on one card, and as Jean read it, the door opened and out came a sandy rabbit, with a pair of big glasses on his nose and a pen behind his ear. Another door had "Mister Miggle" on and Jean longed to know what he was like. But his door remained tight shut.

A third door had "Pixie Lightfeet" on the card outside, and some one was singing a gay little song inside. Jean longed to push the door open and see the pixie, but she didn't dare to.

"Come along come along," said the brownie, who was a most impatient fellow. "We shall miss the Cushion!"

"Cushion!" said Jean, in surprise. "What do you mean by cushion? How can we miss a cushion?"

"Wait and see," said the gnome. "Just hurry up, that's all."

So they hurried on, past all the exciting doors, and at last came to a turn-stile. A big hare sat on a stool there with yellow tickets in a bundle before him. On the other side of the turn-stile was a very large pink cushion.

"Goodness! It's a slide!" said Jean, pointing. "Look! The Cushion is going to slide down that very steep passage. Ooh, what fun! I *shall* hold tight!"

The brownie took two tickets and told the children to sit on the Cushion.

"At the end of the Cushion-Ride you will come to a cave," said the brownie. "Go through it and take the boat you will see waiting. It will take you to the Enchanter's castle if you tell it to. But mind – don't let the Enchanter catch you, for he is a very horrid fellow and will turn you into bars of chocolate and eat you up! Tell the bird you have come from Bindle the Brownie and pull three feathers from her tail."

The children sat down on the great, fat Cushion. A black rabbit, a small pixie, a funny little man with a pointed hat, and a very prickly hedgehog took tickets and scrambled on to the Cushion, too. Jean didn't like sitting next to the hedgehog. His spines stuck into her leg and he wouldn't move even though she asked him to, most politely. She thought he must be deaf.

A bell rang, and the hare sitting by the turnstile cried, "Off you go!" in a very loud voice. He pushed the Cushion and it slid down the steep slide.

Whoooosh! Whoooooosh! Down it went, and the children clutched it tightly. Oh, what a funny feeling it was! They didn't know whether they liked it or not, but it was all most exciting. The hedgehog caught hold of Jean and wouldn't let go.

The little man next to Leslie lost his pointed hat, and he burst into tears and begged Leslie to stop the Cushion and go back for his hat. Leslie told him at least six times that he didn't know *how* to stop the Cushion, and the little man cried tears all down Leslie's leg. Altogether it was very thrilling indeed.

At last the Cushion came to a stop, and every one scrambled off, the little man still sobbing about his lost hat. Jean was glad to see the hedgehog go, for her legs were quite scratched with his prickles.

"Now we'd better look for the boat,' said Leslie, so they walked through the big cave in which they found themselves. It was a queer cave, full of twinkling stones that shone in the walls and in the floor as they walked. These stones lighted up the cave enough for the children to see where they were going.

They walked to the other end of the cave and came to a little chattering stream that ran into a long tunnel. By the side was a tiny boat, shaped like a big fish.

"This must be the boat," said Leslie. "I

say! Isn't this exciting, Jean. Come on, let's get in!"

"All I hope is that Snip-Snap, that Enchanter, doesn't catch us," said Jean. "I don't want to be turned into a bar of chocolate and eaten!"

"I'll look after you," said Leslie. "I'm a boy, and boys can always look after girls if they are in danger."

They got into the fish-boat. "Go to the Enchanter's castle," said Leslie, to the boat. At once it started off down the queer stream and entered the dark tunnel. As it floated into the tunnel its eyes blazed alight, and shone down the stream. In some places the roof of the tunnel was so low that the children had to crouch down in the boat to prevent their heads from being bumped. At last they saw a glimmer of daylight far ahead at the end of the tunnel.

"We're coming out in the open air again!" said Jean. "That's good! I'm getting tired of this darkness!"

They floated out of the tunnel and found themselves in the country-side, on a little blue stream that wound in and out of green fields. At last the fish-boat came to a stop at a small landing stage – and there above them, on a high hill, was the Enchanter's castle. Hundreds of steps led up to it. It was a magnificent castle, with dozens of towers, and a great oak door studded with bright nails.

The children jumped out of the boat, and up the steps they climbed. They were very soon out of breath, for the stairs were steep, and there was no resting-place. So they sat down on the steps to get their breath. Just as they were about to get up again, they heard the sound of a door slamming and they looked up to the castle.

"Gracious! It's the Enchanter himself," cried Leslie in fright. "Look at his pointed hat!"

Jean looked. She saw a tall man in a flowing cloak and big, pointed hat coming down the steps towards them. He had slammed the big wooden door behind him and he seemed to be in a big hurry. The children squeezed themselves to the side of the steps out of his way.

"Out of my way, out of my way!" he cried, in a deep voice. He passed them and went on down to the bottom, where the children lost sight of him.

"Good!" said Leslie, beginning to climb the stairs again. "That means that the Enchanter is out – now we can get the Hoodle Bird's feathers easily, I should think."

When they got to the top of the steps they saw a notice that said: "To the Kitchen Entrance."

"Let's go the kitchen way," said Jean. "The Hoodle Bird might be in the kitchen. I don't want to knock at that great wooden door."

So they took the path that led round to the kitchen – and the Hoodle Bird *was* there! Not in a cage, as they had imagined – but walking about with a shawl round her shoulders, sweeping and dusting!

"Goodness!" said Jean, peeping in at the door. "Is that the Hoodle Bird, do you suppose?"

"Do you want me?" asked the strange bird, coming to the door. Jean saw that the bird had red shoes on its feet, and it waddled like a duck.

"Er – well, we came to ask if we might pull three feathers from your tail," said Leslie.

"Three feathers from my tail!" said the Hoodle Bird, indignantly. "Well, I never! What next!"

"The brownie called Bindle sent me to ask you," said Leslie.

"Oh, he did, did he?" said the bird, and it snapped its beak angrily. "Well, did Bindle send the gooseberry jam he promised?"

"He didn't say anything about gooseberry jam," said Jean, puzzled. "Must you have some?"

"I *must* have a jar of gooseberry jam for my tail-feathers," said the bird. "Bindle knows that. He owes me two jars already, and I'm not going to send him any more feathers till I get a jar of gooseberry jam!"

"But, Hoodle Bird," said Jean, "you see, the Brownie has got our mother's pearl brooch, and he won't give it to us unless

54

we take him back three of your feathers. So do give them to us."

"Get me a jar of gooseberry jam and I will," said the bird. "Though what Snip-Snap will say if he sees my tail short of feathers again, I don't know!"

"But where can we get a jar of gooseberry jam from?" asked Leslie, crossly. "It seems so silly to ask us to get a thing like that. Are there any shops near here?"

"Of course not," said the bird. "You'll have to go to the cottage down the other side of the hill, where Dame Tick-tock lives. She makes all kinds of jam."

"Well, I suppose we *must* go and ask her," said Leslie, and he and Jean went down the path pointed out to them by the Hoodle Bird. Soon they came to a most extraordinary cottage, that turned round and round on a stalk.

"How in the world can we knock at the door of this cottage?" said Jean. "Why, the cottage is turning round so fast that I can hardly see where the door is!"

At that moment the face of an old

woman appeared at one of the windows. She smiled at them and then the cottage turned more and more slowly and at last stopped. The door opened and Dame Tick-tock appeared.

"What do you want?" she asked.

"A jar of your gooseberry jam for the Hoodle Bird," said Leslie, boldly.

"What, does that greedy bird want more gooseberry jam!" cried Dame Tick-tock. "Did she give you a silver penny for it?"

"No," said Leslie, disappointed. "Oh, I say! Have we to pay for it? I've got one penny, but it isn't silver, it's copper."

"Well, get it changed to silver," said the old dame. "Do you see that man bathing in the stream on the hill-side? Go and ask him to change your copper penny into silver and he'll soon manage it for you."

The children saw some one in a yellow bathing costume splashing about in a stream that rippled down the hill-side and made a deep pool near by. They went down the path to the pool and called to the man.

"Would you please change our copper penny into silver for us?"

The man came to the bank and took their penny. "Wait till I get my cloak on," he said. "I can't do magic unless I've got my cloak on, you know."

He picked up a cloak from the grass and flung it round his shoulders – and then, to the children's horror, they saw that he was the Enchanter Snip-Snap himself! He put on his pointed hat too, and smiled down at them. But when he saw how frightened they looked he frowned.

"What's the matter?" he asked. "I shan't eat you!"

"Won't you really?" asked Jean. "The brownie called Bindle told us that you would turn us into bars of chocolate and eat us up if you caught us."

"Oh, he did, did he?" asked Snip-Snap. "Well, I'd certainly do that to *him*, if I caught him, for a ruder, meaner, more dishonest brownie I've never met. Did he send you here?"

"Yes," said Leslie. "You see, he found a pearl brooch that our mother is very fond of, and he wouldn't give it back to us until we came to your castle and took three yellow feathers out of the Hoodle Bird's tail for his new blue hat."

"He doesn't want them for his new hat!" said the Enchanter angrily. "He knows that there is a tremendous lot of magic in the Hoodle Bird's feathers and he wants to make some bad spells. I know Bindle. He's a bad brownie, and he wants a good spanking. Well, did you get the feathers from my Hoodle Bird?"

"No," said Jean. "She said she wanted a jar of gooseberry jam for them, so we went to Dame Tick-tock to get a jar – but she wanted a silver penny for a jar, and as we only had a copper one she told us to go and ask you to change it into silver for us."

"Well, I shan't," said the Enchanter, looking very fierce. "My Hoodle Bird will make herself ill if she gobbles any *more* jam this week, and I won't have it."

"Oh, dear," said Jean, the tears in her eyes. "Now we shan't be able to get back our mother's brooch."

"Cheer up," said the Enchanter. "I'll go
58

back to Bindle with you and make him give up what isn't his, the bad rascal!"

He walked back up the path with them. Dame Tick-tock's cottage had started going round and round again, but as they approached it stopped once more and she came out holding a little jar of gooseberry jam.

"We shan't want it now," said Leslie. She looked so disappointed that the Enchanter suddenly took the copper penny from Leslie's hand and changed it into silver by breathing on it, back and front. It shone brightly, and Leslie pressed it into Dame Tick-tock's hand, and took the jam from her.

"Keep it for yourself," said the Enchanter. "Don't you dare give it to that Hoodle Bird of mine!"

"Oh, no, we won't!" promised Jean. "We should love to take it home to have for our tea."

As they got near the castle they saw the Hoodle Bird looking for them. In her right wing she held three long tail-feathers, ready to give the children – but as soon as she saw the Enchanter she gave a frightened squawk and disappeared into the scullery. Snip-Snap followed her.

"How dare you give away your tail-feathers!" he shouted. "Don't you know that they are magic, and that only I must use them! You greedy bird! You shall have no jam for a month! Give me those feathers."

The Hoodle Bird began to sob and screech and the Enchanter took away the three feathers from her.

"You shall have these feathers for yourselves," he said to the children. "There is a wish in each of them, so be careful how you use them. Now let's go back to that rascally brownie and get your mother's brooch."

"Shall we catch the fish-boat back to the caves?" asked Jean excitedly.

"Bless you, no; there's a quicker way than that!" said the Enchanter. "Come here – under my cloak."

The children went to him and he wrapped them round in his cloak. Then he cried out a long magic word and in a trice all three were lifted into the air and carried along on a strong wind. They were set gently down again at last, and lo and behold, when they peeped out of the cloak they were by the stile near which Mother had lost her pearl brooch!

"Bindle, Bindle!" called Leslie. At once the brownie came running out from beneath his bush – and to his great horror the Enchanter caught him and held him fast!

"Ho, ho!" said Snip-Snap in glee. "So this is the brownie who makes faces at me, is it? This is the brownie who sends children to get the magic feathers from my Hoodle Bird! This is the brownie who steals other people's pearl brooches! Ho, ho! What about turning him into a bar of chocolate and eating him?"

"No, no!" cried the brownie. He pulled the pearl brooch from his pocket and flung it to the children. "Spare me, spare me!"

"Oh, please don't change him into anything and eat him," begged Jean, with tears in her eyes. "He isn't a very nice brownie, and he'd taste horrid – but anyway I couldn't bear to see him changed into chocolate, really I couldn't!"

"Well, I'll spank him instead," said the Enchanter. "You go home now and give your Mother her brooch."

Off they ran, and as they went they heard the bad brownie beginning to howl. "Boo-hoo-hoo! Boo-hoo-hoo!"

He was getting his spanking.

"I really think he deserves it, Jean," said Leslie. And I think he did too, don't you?

As for those magic tail-feathers and the gooseberry jam, goodness knows what exciting things will happen to Leslie and Jean when they eat the jam and use the wishes in the yellow feathers. I wish I was going to be there to see!

4: *Too Clever for Mister Slick*

Jean and Morris had a penny each to spend. They ran off to the sweet-shop, and looked into the window. It was a lovely shop. There were chocolate animals of all kinds, boxes of sweets, dishes of peppermints, toffees, caramels and fruit drops, and, in one corner, little penny bags of sherbert powder.

"I think I'll buy some sherbert," said Morris. "It's such fun to put it into water and make it all go fizzy. It's lovely to drink when it's fizzy, it tickles your nose."

"Well, I'll buy some liquorice," said Jean. "I like the kind that looks like black elastic, just like my garters."

So they went into the shop and bought what they wanted. Morris had a bag of sherbert powder, and Jean had a long piece of liquorice.

"Don't let's eat them till we get home," said Morris. "Then we can think about them all the way."

So they each put their sweet bags in their pockets and walked home. And then their adventures began.

Jean saw the funny motor-car first. It was bright yellow with red spots, and was so small that it really looked more like a very big toy car. In it was a small fat man wearing large motor-goggles and a red leather coat much too tight for him.

He stopped his car just by the children and beckoned to them.

"Hey!" he called. "Which is the way to the Market Gate?"

"Let me see," said Morris. "Well, you want to go down the High Street, then turn to the left by the old clock, then to the right by the river and then when you see a cab-stand you go to the right, and . . . ."

"Oh, my goodness!" said the little fat man. "I can't remember all that! Jump in, both of you, and show me the way. That will be the easiest."

Now both Morris and Jean had been

told that they must NEVER go in a strange motor-car with a strange person, so they knew quite well it was wrong. But they went, all the same. Wasn't it silly of them?

"He'll only take us to the Market Gate, Jean," whispered Morris, as they got in, "and we shall have a lovely ride. It can't matter just for once."

But it did matter, as you will soon see. For when the car got to the Market Gate safely, the driver didn't stop. No, he gave a most peculiar chuckle and drove straight on, past the gate and out into the country.

"Stop!" said Morris. "Here's the gate. Stop!"

"I don't want to stop," said the driver. "I didn't really want to know the way. It was just a trick to get you into the car. Ho, ho! I'm taking you to Caravan Land, where I live, because I want a little girl to do my washing and a little boy to clean my car each day!"

"How wicked of you to trick us like that!" cried Jean. "Stop your car at once and let us get out. If you don't a policeman will come after you!"

"Pooh, I don't believe *that*!" said the driver scornfully. "Anyway, I shan't stop!"

The car went faster than ever! Jean and Morris held on tightly, and the wind whistled through their hair. They had no breath left to say another word.

It was a long drive through country they had never seen before. Once they passed through a pixie town made of big and little toadstools. Another time they passed a towering palace that shone like silver. It was beautiful. Then they came to the strange Land of Caravans.

All the houses were caravans on wheels. They were brightly painted, red, yellow, blue, green – all colours of the rainbow. They had tiny coloured curtains at the windows and little tin chimneys sticking out at the top.

"Here's Caravan Land," said the driver, waving his hand towards the caravans. "All the people who live here are witches, wizards, enchanters and magicians who have been turned out of Fairyland for doing mischief. They have had to leave their palaces and castles, so now they live in caravans and can move about from place to place if the fairy soldiers come chasing after them again."

"What are *you*, then?" asked Jean. "Are you a wizard?"

"I'm half a goblin and half a wizard," said the strange little driver. "My mother was a witch so I know a good deal of magic. I was turned out of Fairyland because I put a spell on the King's boots and they all walked out of the cupboard one morning and never came back. Ho, ho, ho! What a joke!"

"Not very clever," said Morris. "It's the sort of silly thing a fellow like you *would* do!"

"Don't you talk to me like that!" said the driver fiercely. "I'm not silly! I'm a very clever person. If you were half as clever as I am you'd be at the top of your school!"

The queerest people were living in Caravan Land. Witches with cloaks and tall hats walked about, and enchanters went shopping with small rabbits and hares to carry their baskets. The children saw one wizard whose cloak was ten yards long, and a witch whose black cat walked behind her, carrying her basket. It was all very strange, like a dream.

At last the little car stopped opposite a blue caravan with yellow curtains at the window.

"Here we are," said the driver, getting out. "I'm Mister Slick, and this is where I live. Now then, boy, go into the caravan and find a pail. Then get some water and a cloth and clean the car for me. You, girl, can start some washing. There are all the breakfast-things to wash up first. Then you can wash my curtains and my table-cloths."

He bustled the children up the steps, and they had to do as they were told. Soon Morris was cleaning the car and Jean was washing up the breakfast-things.

Mister Slick disappeared to do some shopping. When their jobs were finished the children sat down to rest. Then Jean remembered the strip of black liquorice she had in her pocket. She took it out to nibble.

Some small, goblin-like children came up to look at her. When they saw her nibbling her strip of liquorice they were astonished.

"Look!" they whispered to one another. "She's eating elastic! How clever of her!"

That made Jean laugh. She guessed the goblin children had never seen liquorice-strips before. She was just going to offer them a piece when Mister Slick came back, looking very pleased with himself.

"I've shopped well this morning," he said. "I used some magic money."

He put down a bag of potatoes, sugar, bread and apples.

"What's magic money like?" asked Morris.

Mister Slick grinned. "Oh, it *looks* the same as ordinary money when I give it to the shopman – but as soon as his back is turned it hops out of the shop and runs all the way back to the person who paid for the things. So I get back my money to spend the next day again!"

"But that's cheating!" cried Jean. "How horrid of you! You get the things for nothing then, and when the poor shop-man looks for his money, there isn't any. How horrid you are!"

"It's *not* cheating!" cried Mister Slick angrily. "I'm cleverer than the shop-man, that's all."

"Well, it may be clever, but it's bad," said Morris. "And now, look here, Mister Slick – we've done a lot of work for you, and you had better let us go back home again."

"Well, I shan't then!" said Mister Slick. "I want you for always to clean my car and to do my washing."

"That's silly," said Jean. "You can't keep us like that."

"Oh, can't I!" said Mister Slick. "Well, you'll see!"

"We'll pay you a reward to let us go," said Morris, anxiously.

"If you aren't careful a policeman will come after you from our land," said Jean.

"The only thing that would make me let you go would be if you were cleverer than I am," said Mister Slick, grinning. "Witches and wizards have long since learnt not to keep servants cleverer than they are – but I'm sure there's not a single thing you can do that I can't! And I'm quite sure there are a great many things *I* can do that you can't!"

"Perhaps there are," said Morris. "You do all sorts of nasty cheating things that boys and girls would hate to do – but I'm sure Jean and I can do lots of things *you* can't do, so there!"

"Well, I'll make a bargain with you," said Mister Slick. "If you can do something *I* can't do you shall go free. There! I can't say fairer than that."

"Oh, yes, you could," said Jean sharply, "but you won't. Well, leave me and Morris by ourselves for a few minutes and let us talk. Then we shall soon think of something you can't do!"

"POOH!" shouted Mister Slick rudely, and walked into the caravan and slammed the door, leaving the two children together. They looked at one another anxiously.

"He's horrid," said Morris. "We must trick him somehow, Jean. I wouldn't be his servant for anything."

He put his hands into his pockets and frowned. Then he suddenly felt the bag of sherbert there, the one he had bought at the sweet-shop that morning. He took it out.

"Let's have a little sherbert to drink, Jean," he said. "It might help us to think!"

He took a glass from a shelf outside the caravan and filled it with water. Then he emptied a little of the sherbert into it. It fizzed up at once and frothed over. The goblin children came nearer to watch. When they saw Morris tilt up the glass and drink the water they cried out in astonishment.

"First he made the water boil, and then he drank it when it was boiling!" they cried. "He is a magician! Nobody else could do that!"

"Aren't they funny!" said Jean. "They said I was wonderful to be able to eat liquorice, because they thought it was elastic, and now they think you're marvellous because you drink sherbert! They think you made the water boil – they didn't know it was only sherbert powder that made it fizz up and froth over!"

Morris laughed – and then he suddenly clapped his hands together.

"Jean! We might be able to trick that clever little cheat, Mister Slick! Listen!"

He whispered in Jean's ear and she laughed out loud and nodded her head.

"Yes, we'll do it," she said. "I've got plenty of liquorice left, and you've still got half a bag of sherbert, haven't you?"

Just then the door of the caravan flew open and out came Mister Slick.

"You've had enough time together!" he shouted. "Now then, what can you do that I can't? Nothing, I'm sure!"

"Oh, yes, we can," said Morris at once. "Can you eat elastic?"

"I've never tried," said Mister Slick, looking astonished. "But if you can, I can."

"And can you make a glass of water boil and then drink it?" asked Morris.

Mister Slick looked still more astonished.

"Well," he said, "well-er-yes, I think I could, if you could do it first!"

"Very well, then, watch!" said Jean. She

took out her strip of liquorice and began to eat it. It looked exactly like black garter-elastic, and Mister Slick's eyes nearly fell out of his head with astonishment.

"Never seen that done before," he exclaimed. "But still, if you can do it, I can too!"

He ran into the caravan and came out with a work-basket. He hunted in it and found a piece of black elastic rather like the piece of liquorice that Jean had. She had eaten it nearly all now, and as Mister Slick watched her, she chewed up the very last bit!

"There!" she said. "It's gone! Now let us see *you* eat a piece of elastic, Mister Slick!"

Mister Slick took up his piece of elastic and looked at it doubtfully. It didn't seem a very nice thing to eat. He put one end in his mouth and began to chew.

My goodness, it *was* horrid! He could hardly bear it in his mouth.

"Go on," said Jean. "Eat it up properly,

as I did, Mister Slick. You haven't swallowed any yet."

Well, do you know, poor Mister Slick could *not* swallow that piece of elastic, no matter how much he chewed it. He felt quite ill, and suddenly he turned very green and sat down on the grass.

"I can't do it," he said. "It's dreadful. I'm not clever enough to eat elastic. Little girl, you are cleverer than I am, and so you can go free. I don't want you for a servant. You might put elastic in my soup."

"Oh, I certainly should," said Jean at once. "I might put pins and needles too. But I'm not going to go free unless you let Morris come too."

"Well, he can't go until he has shown that he can do something I can't do," said Mister Slick, feeling a little better. "I must have *one* servant at any rate. He doesn't look as sharp as you, girl, so I dare say I shall be able to keep him."

"Well, look here!" said Morris, taking up his glass. "Can you make the water boil in your glass and then drink it up? Watch me!"

He filled the glass with cold water from a jug and slipped in some sherbert powder at the same time. To Mister Slick's enormous surprise the water fizzed up and frothed over, making a loud bubbling noise as it did so, just like boiling water does. Then Morris tilted up the glass and drank down the whole lot in two or three gulps!

"Oooooh!" said Mister Slick. "Yes, that's clever! You must be half a magician, I should think."

"No, I'm just an ordinary boy," said Morris. "But even · ordinary boys are cleverer than *you*, Mister Slick. Now come along, make a glass of water boil and then drink it!"

Mister Slick filled a glass from the jug of cold water. Then he said all sorts of magic words over it to make it boil. Nothing happened. Then he set it down on the ground, clapped his hands twice, and danced round it six times, singing a magic song. Still nothing happened.

Then he picked it up again, and twisted it cleverly twenty times round his hands, without spilling a drop. And the water began to boil! Yes, it really did! It was real magic, marvellous to watch. The children looked on in surprise. But Morris felt dreadfully disappointed – he didn't want Mister Slick to keep him for a servant, and it looked as if he really were going to make the water boil, and drink it.

At last the water in the glass really was boiling and Mister Slick cried out in delight. Then, just as Morris had done, he tilted up the glass and drank the boiling water.

Oh! How hot it was! He drank one gulp and then shouted out in pain! He flung the half-full glass away and danced round and round, holding his hands to his mouth.

"It's scalded me, it's scalded me!" he howled. "Oh, how I wish I hadn't tried to drink it! Oh, I'm scalded! Oh, my poor mouth!"

The children waited until he had finished dancing about. Then Morris spoke very firmly.

"Well, are you as clever as we are, or

aren't you? Do you still want us for servants?"

"No, a thousand times no!" cried Mister Slick, shaking his head so quickly that his hat flew off. "You are far too clever for me! My goodness, how foolish I was to pick you up in my car! I've tried to eat elastic and it's made me feel very ill. And I've tried to drink boiling water and it's scalded my mouth. No, no, I shall leave children alone after this. They are taught to be too clever nowadays, I can see that! You can go!"

"Well, you'll please take us back home again in your car!" said Jean. "Hurry up, now."

"If you're so clever you can find the way home yourself, surely," said Mister Slick, sulkily.

"Do you want us to show you something even cleverer than we have done yet?" asked Morris, frowning a fearful frown. "Do you want to be turned into a door-mat or changed into a dog-kennel?"

"Oh, my goodness gracious me, can you do that sort of thing too?" cried Mister

Slick, turning very pale and hurrying to his car. "Pray don't try any more clever tricks! I'm frightened, I really am."

He sat down in the driver's seat shaking like a jelly, and Jean saw that tears were pouring down his cheeks. She didn't feel a bit sorry for him. She was very glad to think that for once somebody had frightened *him*! He was always cheating and frightening other people—now he knew what it was like! Good!

They started off in the little red and yellow car, and very soon they had left the funny Land of Caravans far behind. They passed the silvery palace once again and ran through the pixie village of toadstools.

And then at last they were at the Market Gate. "Thank you," said Morris, politely, getting out. "Come on, Jean. We shall have to hurry now. Good-bye, Mister Slick – and mind you never, *never*, NEVER try to run off with children again or you might have to eat elastic and drink boiling water! Ha, ha!"

Mister Slick gave a frightened shout and raced off again, nearly knocking over a lamp-post on the way. To the children's tremendous astonishment the car jumped right over the lamp-post and then tore on again.

"Well, he really *is* clever," said Morris. "But what a nasty little fellow! Come on, Jean, let's go and tell Mother all about it!"

Off they went, and when Mother heard all that had happened she could hardly believe her ears. But all she said was: "Well, what did I tell you? I said that something horrid would happen if you went for a ride in a strange car with a person you didn't know. DON'T DO IT AGAIN!"

I don't think they will, do you? But wasn't it a good thing they bought a strip of liquorice and a bag of sherbert that morning? If they hadn't they might be cleaning and washing for Mister Slick to this very day!

5: *Toy-Town Adventures*

Alison and Morris were going out for a picnic. They had their lunch in a basket, and they meant to go to Windy Hill and eat it there. Windy Hill was a most exciting place. You could see over the fields and lanes for miles around, and if you rolled a stone down it would go bumping along right to the very bottom into the blue stream that curled round the foot of the hill.

"We'll roll some stones down before we eat our lunch," said Morris. "We'll see if we can make one splash into the stream at the bottom!"

So when they got to Windy Hill they found some big stones and sat down to roll them. One by one they bumped down Windy Hill, jumping high in the air as they went. It was great fun.

Alison found an extra big one and rolled it down – and dear me, when it got to some bushes a little way down the hill, they heard a loud yell, and somebody rushed out of the bushes in fright. It was a little man, and he disappeared round the hill, holding one of his arms with his hand.

"My stone hit him!" said Alison, in dismay. "Oh, I say! I didn't know there was any one there! I do hope I haven't hurt him."

"Didn't he look a queer little creature!" said Morris. "Let's go and see if we can find him. We ought to say we're sorry."

They went down the hill-side to the bushes out of which the little man had run, but they couldn't see a sign of him anywhere around – until Morris spied a very strange thing!

It was a small wooden milk-cart, with a wooden horse harnessed in front of it. In the cart were churns of milk.

"Why, it's like a toy milk-cart, just big enough to take children about," said Morris. "Do you suppose it belongs to that little man?"

"I don't know," said Alison. "I say, Morris – let's get into the milk cart for a minute. It would be lovely to pretend it was ours."

The two children got into the little milk-cart, and Morris took the lid off a churn to see if there was really milk inside. And just then, whatever do you think happened? Why, the wooden horse looked round with a frightened face, and called out: "Oh, where's my master!"

The children were so astonished that they could say nothing at all: and suddenly the wooden horse began to gallop down the hill for all he was worth, the milk-cart swinging behind him. The two children clung to the sides in fright, and wondered whatever was going to happen.

Down the hill went the horse, and at last came to an opening in the hill-side. It was a cave, and into it he went at top speed.

"Wherever are we going?" shouted Morris to Alison. "Don't be frightened. I'll look after you!"

The cave narrowed into a passage which was lighted by ball-shaped lamps all the way along. Now and again queer-looking little people flattened themselves against the wall to let the milk-cart pass by, and looked after the children in surprise.

At last the passage came to an end, and the horse galloped into what looked like a small square room. Here he stood still, panting, and the children were just going to get out, when suddenly the little room began to move upwards!

"Oh, it's a lift!" cried Alison in surprise. "Goodness, whatever next? Wherever are we going to?"

Up and up the lift went and at last stopped. Before the children could get out, a large sliding door opened in front of the cart, and out galloped the horse again at top speed, the children holding on to the sides tightly for fear of being shaken out.

And when they looked round they guessed where they were! It was Toy-Town! All the houses were just like dolls' houses; and the shops were exactly like toy sweet-shops. All kinds of toy animals walked about the streets, and in the distance was a toy fort with wooden soldiers parading round the battlements. It was really most exciting!

"I say! What fun!" began Morris, excitedly – but suddenly he stopped. A big stuffed policeman suddenly appeared from somewhere and held up his hand in front of the milk-cart. The wooden horse stopped so quickly that the children fell in a heap on the floor of the cart.

"Now then, now then, what's all this?" said the policeman, taking out a large notebook. "How dare you drive through Toy-Town at this pace? You're breaking the law!"

"We weren't driving. The horse was running away with us," said Morris.

"I was running away because these children don't belong to my milk-cart!" said the wooden horse, suddenly. "They've stolen the cart, and my master is lost and I don't know where he is. Boo-hoo-hoo!"

"Oh, the story-teller!" cried Morris. "We didn't steal the cart! We just got into it and the horse ran off."

"What did you get into it for?" asked the policeman, writing in his notebook.

"Well – just to see how it felt to be in a toy milk-cart," said Alison.

"Seems a funny sort of reason," said the policeman. "I'm afraid you must give me your names and addresses and come with me. I must lock you up until we can find the real owner of the cart and hear what he has to say."

Alison began to cry, but Morris comforted her. "Never mind!" he said. "It's all an adventure, Alison. Think what a fine tale we shall have to tell when we get home again!"

But Alison was really very frightened, especially when the stuffed policeman took out a big silver whistle and blew a loud blast on it. At once all the soldiers on the fort began to march out of the gateway and came in a straight line down the road towards the policeman.

"Are they coming to take us to the fort?" asked Morris.

"Yes," said the policeman. "But don't worry, the soldiers won't do you any harm. We haven't got a police station in Toy-

Town, so prisoners always have to go to the fort with the soldiers."

The toy soldiers surrounded the children and marched them off to the fort. A crowd of dolls and toy animals stood on each side of the road and watched them go, chattering excitedly. Alison dried her tears and looked as brave as she could. She didn't want to cry in front of the toys!

The fort was just like Morris's toy fort at home. There was a sloping passage painted bright red, leading through a gateway. Inside the fort was a big room round which many more wooden soldiers stood, with their guns over their shoulders.

"I suppose they can't sit down because they are made of wood," whispered Morris to Alison. "There aren't any chairs at all!"

The captain sent one of the soldiers to fetch two chairs from the nearest doll's house for the children to sit on. They sat down, and then Morris remembered the picnic basket, which he had carried all the way with him!

"I say, Alison! Let's have something to

eat whilst we're waiting. I'm jolly hungry, aren't you?"

As soon as the toy soldiers saw the sandwiches, cakes, biscuits, chocolate and apples in the basket they crowded round.

"Ooh!" they cried, altogether, and they looked so hungry that the children offered them some of their food.

"Thank you a thousand times!" cried the soldiers. "We only get wood splinters to eat, you know, because we are made of wood, and this food is a real treat. The dolls have sawdust, of course—they are lucky – but, dear me, wouldn't they envy us if they saw us eating this simply scrumptious food!"

In a few minutes all the food was gone, and the wooden soldiers thanked the children again and again for their treat. Just as Alison was brushing the crumbs off her frock, there came a noise outside the fort, and the soldiers all sprang to attention.

"Ho, soldiers! Bring the prisoners to the Town Hall to be tried!" cried the voice of the Captain, and he entered the big room.

All the soldiers saluted, and the two children were marched out of the fort, down the street, and at last came to a wooden building with Town Hall written over the doorway.

Inside, behind a big table, sat a golliwog, looking very stern. In front, sitting on twelve chairs in a wooden compartment, were twelve dolls and animals. They were the jury, who were to judge whether or not the children had done wrong. In another place was a wooden milkman, his hand bound up in a bandage – and the children knew that he was the little man who had been hit by their stone.

"Now," said the golliwog, sternly. "You two children are accused of three things – one, throwing a stone at this milkman. Two, stealing his horse and cart. Three, driving his horse and cart dangerously through the streets of Toy-Town. What have you to say for yourselves?"

"It is all a mistake," said Morris, standing up very straight. "We were on Windy Hill, rolling stones down to the stream at the bottom, and one of them must have hit the poor milkman. It was quite an accident, and we are very sorry. We ran down to tell him we were sorry, and saw his horse and cart. It was such a nice one that we thought we would like to get into it just for a moment."

"The milkman says you stole it," said the golliwog, looking at some notes in front of him.

"Well, we didn't," said Morris, firmly. "The horse took fright and ran away as fast as he could. He didn't stop until the policeman held out his hand in Toy-Town. We were very frightened, I can tell you!"

"Where is the wooden horse?" asked the golliwog. The horse was called for, and, dragging his milk-cart behind him, he came into the hall, looking scared.

"Did you run away, or were you driven away?" asked the golliwog.

"I r-r-r-ran away!" stammered the horse.

"Did the children whip you, or behave unkindly to you?" asked the golliwog.

"N-n-n-no!" said the horse. "They didn't d-d-d-do anything except st-st-st-stand in the c-c-c-cart!"

"Ha!" said the golliwog, crossing something out in his notebook. "It looks as if the children really didn't mean any harm; they were just meddlesome."

"Please!" said the wooden milkman, popping up. "I think they are unkind, cruel children. They hurt my hand with their stone!"

"Can anyone say whether or not these children are kind or unkind?" asked the golliwog, looking round the court... and all at once every single one of the wooden soldiers who were in the court shouted at the top of their voices:

"They're kind, they're kind! They shared their dinner with us, and it was the most scrumptious food we have ever tasted!"

What a noise they made! The golliwog banged on the table with his fist and at last the soldiers were quiet.

"Well, if the children really did share their dinner with the soldiers, it proves they are kind!" said the golliwog. "What do you say, dolls and animals of the jury?"

"We say the same!" cried all the dolls

and animals, jumping up and waving their hands and paws in the air.

The little milkman shouted too, and it seemed as if every one in the hall was going quite mad!

"Let them go, they're kind! Let them go, they're kind!" cried everybody. Then the golliwog got out of his seat, and went solemnly over to the children. He shook hands with them, and told them they were free.

"The milkman will be pleased to drive you all the way home in his cart," he said. "He has quite forgiven you for everything."

"Thank you," said Alison, and Morris added: "We'll come back again another day and bring all sorts of nice things for you to eat!"

Then everybody yelled again and Alison and Morris were taken out to where the milk-cart stood beside the pavement outside. The golliwog shook hands with them again, and off they went, the milkman driving in fine style.

It wasn't very long before they were at

their front gate, and they thanked the milkman very much.

"We hope your hand will soon be better," said Morris, politely.

"Oh, the brownie who lives in the hillside near those bushes bound it up beautifully for me," said the milkman with a smile. "It will soon be all right. Good-bye."

The children ran indoors to tell their mother where they had been, and they begged her to come out and see the wooden milkman and his cart – but he had driven off, and all they could see was a cloud of dust in the distance.

"We're going to Toy-Town again, and we're going to take a great big basket of lovely things to eat!" said Morris, when they had finished telling Mother all their adventures.

"You certainly shall," said Mother. "I can't bear to think of those dolls and soldiers eating wooden splinters and sawdust, poor things! We'll go next week!"

I *do* wish I was going with them, don't you?

6: *The Enchanted Cushion*

Eileen and Denis were very cross with Nurse. They had been building a fine brick house on the nursery floor, and Nurse had made them take it down before they went out.

"Why can't we leave it till we come in?" asked Eileen, crossly. "It won't be in any one's way."

"Well, you *can't* leave it," said Nurse. "When you come in you'll want to play trains or dolls and then all the bricks will be left over the floor. You'll please put them away at once."

The children put them away, grumbling. They didn't want to go out at all, although they were going to the market, which was always a most exciting place. Soon they were ready, and Nurse marched them out into the road.

"When we get to the market, let's give Nurse the slip!" whispered naughty Denis to Eileen. "We'll go round the back of the market, and Nurse won't know where we are!"

So when they came to the market, and Nurse was buying butter at the butter-woman's stall, the two children slipped away. They ran behind the stalls and came out into a rubbish-yard. They ran through a passage and followed it until it came out into another square – and, dear me, there was another market going on in that square!

But what a queer market! And what strange men and women there were at the stalls! They had pointed ears and queer slanting eyes that twinkled like stars. Their tunics and dresses were strange, and very brightly coloured. They stared at the two children and seemed very much astonished to see them.

"Ooh!" said Eileen, her eyes open very wide. "What a funny place! And what funny people!"

"They seem more like fairy folk than

real people," said Denis, in a whisper. "Oh, Eileen – fancy there being a market-place like this so near to the other one!"

"What will you buy, maid and master?" asked a queer-looking little man, whose cap had two holes in it to let his pointed ears through.

"I – I d-d-don't think we w-w-want anything," said Eileen, rather frightened, for his eyes were so very, *very* bright.

"Not *anything*!" said the little man, and he frowned so fiercely that Eileen wanted to run away. "Then why do you come to our market? Perhaps you have come to *sell* something!"

"No," said Denis. "We've only come here by mistake. We'll go back now, thank you very much."

But the little man wouldn't let them go. He caught hold of their hands and held them fast.

"You must buy something before you leave," he said. "It is the rule here."

"I've only got a silver sixpence," said Denis, and he pulled it out of his pocket.

He looked at the nearest stall. It had nothing but gay cushions on it.

"Buy a cushion for the nursery chair," whispered Eileen. "Then let's go, quickly, before these funny people get angry with us."

"Can I have a cushion for my sixpence?" asked Denis, going up to the stall.

"Yes. Choose which you like," answered the old woman behind. She had pointed ears, too, like all the rest, and her eyes were as green as a cucumber. Denis hastily picked up a bright yellow cushion with red spots all over it, and put his sixpence down on the stall.

Then he and Eileen ran out of the market square as fast as they could go.

"They were fairies, as sure as anything!" said Eileen, when at last they came out in a street they knew. "Did you see their pointed ears? Goodness, I thought they were going to keep us there, didn't you?"

"Look, there's Nurse, still buying butter!" said Denis. "She hasn't missed us. Come on, let's go over to her. Don't say anything about that fairy market, because she will only say we're telling stories."

They ran over to Nurse, who was just paying for the butter and eggs she had bought. She took the two children by the hand and off they went home, Denis carrying the cushion under his arm.

"Did you get that whilst we were out?" asked Nurse, in surprise. "Well, it will do nicely for the big nursery chair!" When they got home, the two children sat on the cushion in turn to see if it felt any different from an ordinary cushion.

"Let's wish a wish and see if it does anything!" said Denis. "I'll sit on it and wish."

He sat down on the cushion in the chair. "I wish I was at the bottom of the garden!" he said.

Whiz-z-z-z! Out of the window flew the cushion, with Denis clutching the sides tightly. Goodness, there certainly was magic in that cushion!

Eileen could hardly believe her eyes! She ran down to the bottom of the garden to see if the cushion had really taken Denis there – and sure enough it had! There he was, still sitting on the cushion, looking most astonished!

"I say! It's an enchanted cushion! What fun! Let's take it back to the nursery and play with it!"

Back they went to the nursery, and there they found Nurse, looking very cross.

"Where have you two been? I've been looking for you *every*where! Don't you know it is dinner-time? Wash your hands at once and get ready."

The children popped the cushion into the nursery chair, and did as they were told. They sat down to dinner, but they didn't feel a bit hungry, they were so excited. And, of course, when the rice pudding came in, they neither of them felt that they wanted any!

"I don't want any, Nurse," said Denis.

"Nor do I!" said Eileen. But Nurse took not a bit of notice – she simply handed them their plates of rice pudding and told them to eat it.

Then they began to be naughty, and they just *wouldn't* eat it! They sat there, sulking, and Nurse was very annoyed.

"I can't think what's the matter with you," she said, at last. "Well, I'm not going to sit here any longer at the table, waiting for you. You'll just finish your pudding, and then you can get up. If you don't hurry, you won't be able to go out to tea this afternoon."

Nurse got up and went to sit down on the nursery chair. The new cushion was there, and she sat on it. The children sat with sulky red faces at the table, quite determined not to eat their rice pudding. They looked at one another, and dear me, how cross they felt with Nurse!

Suddenly they heard a gentle snore! Nurse had fallen asleep in the chair! Denis looked at her crossly.

"I wish she was on a little island in the very middle of the sea!" he whispered to Eileen. "She's so . . ."

Then both children gave a loud scream. The cushion in the chair suddenly rose up with their sleeping nurse on it, and flew out of the window!

"Oh, oh! You forgot the enchanted cushion, Denis," cried Eileen, in a fright.

"Look what's happened! Nurse has been taken away, and I'm sure she'll go to a lonely island in the middle of the sea!"

Denis was frightened and upset. He had felt cross with Nurse, but he was very fond of her, and he didn't like to think he had made her disappear like that.

"Whatever will she think when she wakes up and finds herself on an island?" he said. "Oh, Eileen – poor Nurse! I do wish I hadn't said that unkind wish!"

"What are we going to do?" asked Eileen. "Nobody will believe us if we tell them what has happened. But we *must* do something about Nurse!"

"Let's go back and find the market where we bought that cushion," said Denis. "Maybe the queer folk there will tell us what to do."

So they put on their hats and ran down the street to the market-square. They found the little passage that led to the fairy market and went down it. Sure enough, there was the strange market just as before. The queer little people with their pointed ears stared at the two children in surprise.

"What have you come here again for?" asked a little man in yellow, with long pointed shoes on his feet.

"Oh," said Eileen, with tears in her eyes, "you know that cushion we bought, don't you? Well, it was enchanted, and, oh dear, when our nurse sat on it, Denis wished she was away on an island in the very middle of the sea – and now she's gone! And we want to know how to get her back."

All the little folk crowded round the two children, and talked at the tops of their voices. How they chattered! Eileen and Denis couldn't understand a word, because it was pixie-language they spoke, but presently the little fellow in yellow made all the others stay quiet, and then he turned to the waiting children.

"We will go and seek your nurse on the flying donkey," he said. "Would you like to come too?"

"Ooh, yes!" cried the children, in excitement. "Oh, you *are* kind. Where is the donkey?"

The yellow man led the way to the other

102

end of the square, and there, tied up to a post, was a little donkey. But what a strange one! He was yellow, with a blue tail and blue ears! He had big blue wings that grew out of his back, and blue shoes on his feet. The children couldn't believe he was real – but he was, because he suddenly gave a very loud hee-haw that made them jump!

"Here's the flying donkey," said the man in yellow. "You had better get on in front of me, you two children."

Up they got, and then the fairy man got up behind them. "Heyo!" he cried to the donkey, and up in the air the little creature went, flapping his big blue wings.

It *was* exciting! Denis and Eileen held on tightly, and shouted in delight. It was lovely to be high up in the air, and to see all the houses and fields down below, ever so small. The donkey began to go very fast indeed – so fast that the children shut their eyes and held their breath. They couldn't see anything now, even if they did look down, for they were over the sea.

"Perhaps we shall get to an island soon," shouted Denis to Eileen.

"There's one just below us!" said the fairy man. The yellow donkey slowed down, and began to drop gently towards a little green island lying in the blue sea. His wings flapped more and more slowly, and at last he landed.

"Stay here," said the fairy man, jumping off. "I'll soon see if your nurse is here."

He came back in a few moments, shaking his head. Then off they went again, high into the air. After a while they saw another island, and down they dropped.

Time after time they landed on little islands, and the fairy man went to see if their nurse was there, but each time he came back shaking his head. The children were in despair.

"Don't worry," said the little man. "I expect we shall find her soon. The next island is a very favourite one for magic carpets, mats or cushions! She may be there!"

The donkey soon flew down to another little island, and the fairy man jumped off and went away to look for the nurse. When he was gone, the children sat still looking at the feathery trees and brilliant flowers around.

And suddenly they heard a funny noise! They looked this way and that, but couldn't see anything at all.

"What is it?" whispered Denis.

"It sounds like some one snoring," whispered back Eileen. "Oh, Denis – do you suppose it's Nurse?"

"Let's go and look," said Denis, and the two children slipped off the yellow donkey and ran round the bushes to see what the noise was.

And, dear me, would you believe it, there was Nurse! She was sitting on the enchanted cushion, still fast asleep and snoring! All round her grew wonderful flowers, and four brightly coloured squirrels sat in a near by tree and watched her in surprise.

"Ooh, look!" said Eileen, pointing. "There's Nurse! Oh, I *am* glad!"

"And she's still asleep, so if only we can get her back to the nursery without waking, she will never know she was taken away to this island in the middle of the sea!" said Denis.

Just then up came the fairy man, and he stared in astonishment at the sleeping nurse.

"Don't wake her!" whispered Denis. "We're going to wish her back to the nursery!"

The little man nodded. He leaned against a tree and watched.

"I wish Nurse was back in the nursery, still asleep!" said Denis. At once the enchanted cushion rose up into the air with nurse on it, and flew westwards as fast as it could go. Soon Nurse was only a tiny speck in the sky.

"I hope she won't fall off," said Eileen, anxiously.

"Oh, no!" said the fairy man. "She'll be all right Hurry up, now, jump on the flying donkey again, or you won't be back home till long after your nurse has arrived!"

They climbed on to the back of the yellow donkey once more, and away they went. It didn't seem very long before they were back in the market-square again. They jumped off the donkey, patted him, and said thank you very much to his master, the little yellow man.

"We'd better go straight home now," said Eileen. "If Nurse wakes up before we're back we shall get into trouble!"

They ran all the way back home, and were glad to see that Nurse was still asleep when they crept into the nursery. Eileen looked at the clock, and then pointed at it in astonishment.

"We've only been ten minutes!" she said, in a whisper.

"Time in Fairyland is different from here," said Denis. "I say! Let's eat up our rice pudding now. I feel hungry."

They sat down at the table and in a few minutes every scrap of the rice pudding had disappeared! Then suddenly Nurse opened her eyes and looked at them.

"There's good children," she said. "I'm glad you've finished your pudding. Dear me, I do feel sleepy!"

"You've been fast asleep and snoring, Nurse," said Eileen.

'Oh, no, I'm sure I haven't been to sleep," said Nurse, rubbing her eyes. "I just closed my eyes for a moment, but I feel certain I didn't go to sleep."

"But, Nurse, you did, really," said Denis. "Why, you've been on an island in the very middle of the sea, and we went to rescue you on a yellow donkey with blue wings!"

"Don't talk nonsense," said Nurse. "Yellow donkey with blue wings! Whatever next!"

"Well, we'll *show* you if you like!" said Eileen, jumping up. "Come on, Nurse, it's in a wonderful fairy market, not very far from our own market-place. Oh, do come – truly and really there's a yellow donkey there!"

Nurse was dragged out of the house and down the street with both the children talking at once, telling her all that had happened. She laughed at them, but they were both so serious that she really didn't know *what* to think!

But wasn't it a pity – when the children got to the market-place they couldn't find the little passage that led to the fairy market! It was quite gone. They hunted here and hunted there, but it wasn't a bit of good. They couldn't find it anywhere!

"Oh, what a pity!" cried Denis, vexed. "But never mind! We'll show you what that magic cushion can do, Nurse! Come back home and I'll sit on it and wish myself at the bottom of the garden!"

They all went home – but, oh my, when they ran into the nursery, they found that Tinker the puppy had been there – and he had taken the enchanted cushion from the chair and torn it into bits with his teeth! The pieces were all strewn over the floor!

"Oh, dear, there won't be any magic in it at all, now!" cried Eileen, disappointed. "Look what Tinker's done!"

She picked up the bits, and Nurse fetched a brush and pan to sweep up the feathers that had leaked out from the cushion. They were queer little feathers, bright red with yellow tips, and Nurse said she had never in her life seen any like them before.

"You do believe you were taken away, to a little island in the very middle of the sea and were rescued by me and Denis on a flying donkey, don't you?" said Eileen to Nurse. But Nurse shook her head.

"I couldn't believe a story like that!" she said, laughing. "You show me that fairy market and I'll believe it all – but not till then!"

So every day the children look for the passage that leads to the fairy market – but they haven't found it yet!

Books by **Enid Blyton** for younger readers.

D281

All these books are available at your local bookshop or newsagent, and can be ordered direct from the publisher.

To order direct from the publisher just tick the titles you want and fill in the form below:

Name _____

Address _____

_____

Send to:
Granada Cash Sales
PO Box 11, Falmouth, Cornwall TR10 9EN

Please enclose remittance to the value of the cover price plus:

UK 45p for the first book, 20p for the second book plus 14p per copy for each additional book ordered to a maximum charge of £1.63.

BFPO and Eire 45p for the first book, 20p for the second book plus 14p per copy for the next 7 books, thereafter 8p per book.

Overseas 75p for the first book and 21p for each additional book.

Granada Publishing reserve the right to show new retail prices on covers, which may differ from those previously advertised in the text or elsewhere.